ISBN 0 86112 070 1
This edition published 1990
Printed in Portugal By Edições ASA

NOW YOU CAN READ
·STORIES·

ADAPTED BY LUCY KINCAID

ILLUSTRATED BY ERIC ROWE · BELINDA LYON · CLIVE SPONG

BRIMAX BOOKS · NEWMARKET · ENGLAND

CONTENTS

Little Red Riding Hood

Little Red Riding Hood's mother was packing a basket with eggs and butter and homemade bread. "Who is that for?" asked Little Red Riding Hood.

"For Grandma," said Mother. "She has not been feeling well." Grandma lived alone in a cottage in the middle of the wood.

"I will take it to her," said Little Red Riding Hood. She put on her red cape with the red hood and picked up the basket.

"Make sure you go straight to the cottage," said Mother as she waved goodbye. "And do not talk to any strangers."

Little Red Riding Hood meant to go straight to the cottage but there were so many wild flowers growing in the wood, she decided to stop and pick some for Grandma. Grandma liked flowers. They would cheer her up.

"Good morning," said a voice at her elbow. It was a wolf. "Where are you taking these goodies?" he asked, peeping inside the basket.

"I am taking them to my Grandma," said Little Red Riding Hood, quite forgetting what her mother had said about talking to strangers. "Lucky Grandma," said the wolf. "Where does she live?"

"In the cottage in the middle of the wood," said Little Red Riding Hood.

"Be sure to pick her a nice BIG bunch of flowers," said the wolf, and hurried away.

The wolf went
straight to
Grandma's cottage.
He knocked at the
door.
"Who is there?"
called Grandma.
"It is I, Little
Red Riding Hood,"
replied the wolf
in a 'little girl'
voice.
"Then lift up the
latch and come in,"
called Grandma.

Grandma screamed loudly when she saw the wolf's face peering round the door. He was licking his lips. She jumped out of bed and into the cupboard, and locked herself in.

The wolf picked up her frilly bed-
cap, which had fallen to the floor,
and put it on his own head. He
pushed his ears inside the cap
then climbed into Grandma's bed.
He pulled the covers up round his
neck, then sat and waited for
Little Red Riding Hood to come.

Presently, there was a knock at the door.

"Who is there?" he called, in a voice that sounded like Grandma's.

"It is I, Little Red Riding Hood," replied Little Red Riding Hood.

"Then lift up the latch and come in," called the sly, old wolf.

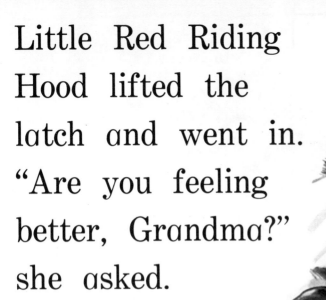

Little Red Riding Hood lifted the latch and went in. "Are you feeling better, Grandma?" she asked.

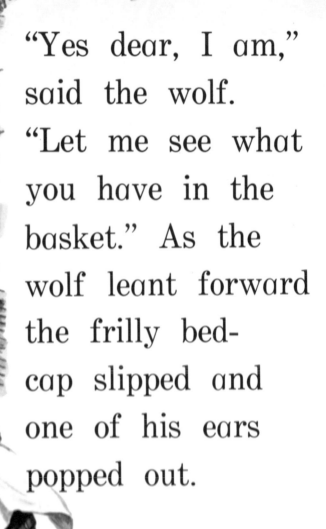

"Yes dear, I am," said the wolf. "Let me see what you have in the basket." As the wolf leant forward the frilly bed-cap slipped and one of his ears popped out.

"What big ears you have," said Little Red Riding Hood.

"All the better to hear you with my dear," said the wolf, turning towards her.

"What big eyes you have," said Little Red Riding Hood, beginning to feel just a tiny bit frightened. "All the better to see you with," said the wolf, with a big grin.

"What big teeth you have," said Little Red Riding Hood, now feeling very frightened indeed.

"All the better to EAT you with,"
said the wolf and he threw back
the covers and jumped out of bed.

"You are not my Grandma!"
screamed Little Red Riding Hood.

"No, I am not. I am the big bad
wolf," growled the wolf in his own
voice. "And I am going to eat
you up."

"Help! Help!" screamed Little Red
Riding Hood as the wolf chased her
out of the cottage and into the
wood.

The woodcutter heard her screams and came to the rescue. As soon as the wolf saw the woodcutter's big wood-cutting axe, he put his tail between his legs and ran away as fast as he could.

Little Red Riding Hood told the woodcutter what had happened. "Where is your Grandma now?" asked the woodcutter.

"I do not know," sobbed Little Red Riding Hood. "Perhaps that horrid wolf has eaten her."

But when they got back to the cottage, they heard the sound of knocking coming from inside the cupboard and a voice asking if it was safe to come out.

"It is me Grandma!" called Little Red Riding Hood.
Only when Grandma was REALLY sure, did she unlock the cupboard door.
"What a lucky escape we have both had," said Little Red Riding Hood as she hugged Grandma.

What a lucky escape indeed.

All these appear in the pages of the story. Can you find them?

Mother

Little Red Riding Hood

Grandma

flowers

wolf

basket

frilly bed-cap

woodcutter

Use the pictures to tell the story
in your own words, and then draw
your own pictures.

Three Little Pigs

Once upon a time there were three
little pigs. One day, their mother
said, "You are old enough to look
after yourselves now. It is time
for you to go out into the world
and build homes of your own."

The three little pigs were very excited. They walked together as far as the crossroads and there they parted.

"Goodbye!" they called to one another as they set off in different directions.

The first little pig always did
things in a hurry. He built himself
a house of straw in the first sunny
field he came to. It was light
and airy and smelt of harvest time
and it swayed gently whenever the

wind blew.
One day he saw a
wicked old wolf
walking across the
field.
"OOOH!" cried the
first little pig
and ran inside his
house of straw.
The wolf knocked
at the door and
called, "Open the
door little pig
and let me in."
He wanted the
little pig for
his dinner.

The first little pig shivered and shook. "By the hair on my chinny chin chin, I will NOT open the door and let you come in."
"Then I will HUFF and I will PUFF and I will blow your house down," growled the wolf.

And he HUFFED and he PUFFED until the house of straw blew away. And THAT was the end of the first little pig.

The second little pig never quite finished anything he started. He built himself a house of sticks in a shady wood. It was full of gaps and creaked whenever the wind blew.

One day he saw a wicked old wolf walking along the woodland path. "OOOH!" cried the second little pig and ran inside his house of sticks. The wolf knocked at the door and called, "Open the door little pig and let me in." He wanted the little pig for his dinner.

The second little pig shivered and shook. "By the hair on my chinny chin chin, I will NOT open the door and let you come in."

"Then I will HUFF and I will PUFF and I will blow your house down," growled the wolf.
And he HUFFED and he PUFFED until the house of sticks tumbled down. And THAT was the end of the second little pig.

The third little
pig always did
everything properly,
even if it took
him a long time.
He built a house
of bricks at the
bottom of a steep
hill. It was snug
and warm and stood
firm and strong.

One day he saw a wicked old wolf walking down the hill.

"OOOH!" cried the third little pig and ran inside his house of bricks. The wolf knocked at the door and called, "Open the door little pig and let me in." He wanted the little pig for his dinner.

The third little pig shivered and shook. "By the hair on my chinny chin chin, I will NOT open the door and let you come in."
"Then I will HUFF and I will PUFF and I will blow your house down," growled the wolf.

And he HUFFED and he PUFFED and then he HUFFED and PUFFED again.

The wicked old wolf HUFFED and he PUFFED until he was quite out of breath but the house of bricks stood as firm and as strong as a mountain. He could NOT blow it down. If he wanted to catch the little pig he would have to entice him out of the house.

"Little pig," he called. "Meet me in the orchard at ten o'clock tomorrow morning and I will show you where the best apples are."

The third little
pig knew how
crafty and full
of tricks the old
wolf was so the
next morning he
got up very early.
He went to the
orchard and picked
all the best
apples and was
safely home again
by ten o'clock.

When the wicked old wolf got to the orchard and found the best apples gone he knew the third little pig had tricked him. He was very angry but he tried not to show it. He went back to the house of bricks and knocked at the door.

"Are you going to market tomorrow?" he called in his most sly voice.

"Yes I am," said the little pig.

"Then I will meet you at eight o'clock and we can walk there together," said the wolf. "Do not be late."

The third little pig got up very early indeed the next morning. "I will be home from market before the old wolf is even awake," he said. But he was wrong because the wolf got up early too.

The little pig was very frightened when he saw the wolf coming up the hill and he hid inside an empty milk churn which was standing beside the road.

The milk churn began to roll. It rolled down the hill. Faster and faster and faster. It bumped right into the old wolf and sent him sprawling.

"OOOH!" cried the wolf. He could not believe his eyes when he saw the little pig hop from the milk churn and run into the house of bricks and slam the door.

He was very angry indeed. If he could not catch the little pig outside the house then he would have to get into the house. If the little pig would not let him in through the door then he would go down the chimney.

The third little pig heard the wolf scrambling about on the roof.

"That wicked wolf will NEVER catch me," he cried. He put a pot full of water on the fire and waited. The rumbling and grumbling in the chimney got louder and then suddenly there was a great BIG SPLASH! The wicked old wolf had fallen straight into the pot. And THAT was the end of HIM.

And the third little pig lived happily ever after.

All these appear in the pages
of the story. Can you find them?

three little pigs

wolf

house of straw

house of sticks

house of bricks

apple

milk churn

pot of water

Use the pictures to tell the story in your own words, and then draw your own pictures.

Goldilocks and the Three Bears

Once upon a time there was a father bear, a mother bear, and a baby bear. They lived together in a little cottage in the middle of a wood. Every morning Mother Bear made porridge for breakfast. One morning the porridge was very hot. "Let us go for a walk in the wood while the porridge cools," said Father Bear.

Mother Bear put on her bonnet and out they went into the sunshine.

re

They pulled the cottage door shut
behind them but it did not latch
properly and presently it swung open.

Goldilocks was out in the wood too that morning. Presently she came to the clearing where the bears' cottage stood. She ran to the open door and peeped inside. "Is there anyone at home?" she called.

She could see that the table was laid for breakfast. She could see thin wisps of steam curling from the three bowls. She wondered what was in them.

"I will go in and take a quick peep and then come out again," she said. "No one will ever know."

She tiptoed across to the table.

Goldilocks was a greedy little girl. When she saw the bowls were full of porridge she picked up a spoon. "I will take just a tiny bit," she said. "No one will ever know." And she took a spoonful of porridge from the largest bowl.

It was very salty.

She did not like it at all.

She took a spoonful of porridge from the middle size bowl.

That was far too sweet.

She did not like that either.

And then she took a spoonful of porridge from the smallest bowl.
It was neither too salty nor too sweet.
It was just right.
And that naughty girl ate it ALL.

There were three wooden chairs with bright patchwork cushions on the seats, beside the fireplace.
Goldilocks decided to try those too.
She sat on the largest chair first.
It was very hard.
She did not like it at all.
She tried the middle size chair.
That was far too soft.
She did not like that either.

And then she tried the smallest chair. It was neither too hard nor too soft. It was just right. But that naughty little girl was NOT right for the chair. She was far too heavy and she wriggled far too much and the little chair broke.

Goldilocks picked
herself up from
the floor and went
up the winding
stairs. There
were three beds
in the bedroom.
A large one,
a middle size one
and a small one.
She tried the large bed first.
It was very hard.
She did not like it at all.
She tried the middle size bed.
That was far too soft.
She did not like that either.
And then she tried the smallest

bed. It was neither too hard nor
too soft. It was just right.
And that naughty little girl curled
up on the bed and went to sleep.

When the three
bears came home
they knew at once
that something was
wrong.
"Someone has been
tasting my porridge,"
growled Father Bear
with his loud, gruff
voice.

"Someone has been tasting my
porridge too," said Mother Bear
with her soft, gruff voice.

"Someone has been tasting MY porridge," said Baby Bear with his tiny, gruff voice. "And what is more they have eaten it all UP." And poor little Baby Bear burst into tears.

65

Mother Bear mopped Baby Bear's tears dry and Father Bear sat down on his chair to think what was to be done. He jumped up at once. "Someone has been sitting on my chair," he growled with his loud, gruff voice.

"Someone has been sitting on my chair too," growled Mother Bear with her soft, gruff voice.

"Someone has been sitting on MY chair," said Baby Bear in his soft, gruff voice. "And what is more they have broken it." And poor Baby Bear burst into tears all over again.

It made Father Bear and Mother Bear very angry indeed to see Baby Bear cry.

When Mother Bear had mopped Baby Bear's tears dry all over again and when Father Bear had promised to mend the broken chair they all went upstairs to make sure nothing else had been broken.

"Someone has been lying on my bed," growled Father Bear with his loud, gruff voice.

"Someone has been lying on my bed
too," growled Mother Bear with her
soft, gruff voice.

"Someone has been lying on MY bed,"
said Baby Bear with his tiny, gruff
voice. "And what is more . . . she is
still there . . . LOOK!"

At that very
moment Goldilocks
woke up and saw
the three bears
looking at her.
She jumped from
the little bed
and ran down the
winding stairs and
out of the cottage
as fast as her
legs would take
her. She did not
stop running until
she got home.

From that day onwards the three bears always made sure the cottage door was firmly closed behind them when they went out. They did not want any more uninvited guests eating their porridge, breaking their chairs or sleeping in their beds.

All these appear in the pages
of the story. Can you find them?

cottage

Father Bear

Mother Bear

Baby Bear

Goldilocks

porridge bowls

chair

bed

Use the pictures to tell the story
in your own words, and then draw
your own pictures.

Jack and the Beanstalk

Jack and his mother were very poor, and one day, Jack's mother sent him to market to sell their only cow. On the way there he met a man who stopped him and said, "Is your cow for sale?"

"Yes," said Jack.

"Then I will give you five beans for her," said the man.

"That does not seem very much to give for a cow," said Jack.

"But they are not just beans," said the man, "they are magic beans."

"Then I will take them, and you may have the cow," said Jack.

When Jack got home he showed his
mother the beans. She was so
cross she snatched them from his
hand and threw them out of the
window. She would not listen when
Jack said they were magic beans.
"There is no such thing as a
magic bean," she said, and she
sent Jack to bed without any
supper.

How wrong she was.
The beans sprouted
in the night and
grew and grew and
GREW. Next
morning there was
an ENORMOUS
beanstalk growing
outside the window.
"I am going to
see what is at
the top," said
Jack and he began
to climb.
"Do be careful,"
called his mother.

Jack climbed and climbed, higher and still higher, until at last he reached a world above the clouds. He knocked at the first door he came to. It was opened by the wife of a giant. She invited Jack into the house for breakfast.

Jack had just finished eating when
he heard the sound of heavy feet
and a loud voice shouting,

"FEE FI FO FUM,
I SMELL THE BLOOD
OF AN ENGLISHMAN!"

"Quick! Quick!" said the woman.
"That is my husband, the giant.
He eats boys like you for his
breakfast. Quick! Quick! Hide
in the oven."
So, of course,
Jack did. HE
did not want
to be eaten.

The giant was
sure he could
smell a boy but
he could not find
him, so he had
to make do with
oatmeal for his
breakfast.

When the giant had scraped his
plate clean he called for his hen.
Jack was peeping from the oven so
he saw what happened next.
"Lay hen!" ordered the giant. And
straight away the hen laid a
beautiful golden egg.

"Mother would like to own a hen
like that," thought Jack.

Jack waited until the giant was
asleep, then he crept from his
hiding place. He picked up the
little hen and tucked it inside
his shirt. "You are coming home
with me," he said.

He ran from the
house without
waking the giant
and climbed down
the beanstalk.
"Look what I
have," he called
as his mother
came to meet
him.

Next morning Jack climbed up the beanstalk again, and went back to the giant's house.

"FEE FI FO FUM!" roared the giant.

"I SMELL THE BLOOD OF AN ENGLISHMAN!"

This time Jack hid in a drawer and the giant had to make do with oatmeal for his breakfast again. It made him very cross.

When the giant had finished his oatmeal, he called for his harp. "Sing harp!" he ordered. And the harp sang though the giant did not touch its strings once.

"Mother would like a harp that sings by itself," thought Jack.

At last the giant fell asleep, and
Jack crept from his hiding place.
He reached out his hand to pick
up the harp, but as soon as he
touched it the harp called loudly,
"Master! Master! Wake up!"
Jack quickly pushed the harp into
his shirt to muffle its voice,
but he was too late.
The giant jumped
from his chair
with a loud roar.

"FEE FI FO FUM!"
he cried, "I KNEW
I COULD SMELL THE
BLOOD OF AN
ENGLISHMAN!"

Jack dodged between the giant's
fingers and ran as fast as he
could to the top of the beanstalk.
"FEE FI FO FUM!" shouted the
giant. He was in a terrible rage.
"FEE FI FO FUM!"

As Jack climbed down the beanstalk he could feel it shaking and trembling. He could feel the giant's breath blowing like a hot fierce wind down his neck. "FEE FI FO FUM!"

Jack's mother heard all the noise and came running. She was very frightened when she saw the giant. "Quick! Quick! Give me the axe!" shouted Jack as he jumped the last few feet to the ground. There was no time to lose. He took the axe from his mother, and with one mighty blow he cut right through the beanstalk.

It fell to the ground with a
great crash, and made a hole so
deep that neither the beanstalk nor
the giant were ever seen again.

As for Jack and his mother, they
lived happily ever after, and with
a hen that laid golden eggs and
a harp that sang by itself they
were never poor again.

All these appear in the pages of the story. Can you find them?

cow

oven

Jack

beanstalk

giant

hen

harp

axe

Use the pictures to tell the story
in your own words, and then draw
your own pictures.

The Gingerbread Man

Once upon a time there was a
little old man and a little old
woman who lived on a farm.
The little old woman liked
cooking and one day, when the
little old man was asleep in his
rocking chair, she had an idea.

"I will make a little gingerbread man," she said. She set to
work at once. She mixed him with
milk and flavoured him with ginger.
She gave him a head and arms and
legs. She gave him two currant
eyes and a candy-peel mouth and
then she put him into the oven.

When it was time to take the gingerbread man out of the oven she woke the old man. "Come and see what I have cooked," she called, as she opened the oven door.

Before she could lift the baking tray from the shelf the gingerbread man had jumped out of the oven by himself.

The old woman screamed and the old man stared in astonishment as the little gingerbread man ran towards the door.

"Stop! Stop!" cried the little old
man and the little old woman as
they ran after the gingerbread man.

"Run, run as fast as you can.
You will never catch me. I am
the gingerbread man," laughed the
gingerbread man. He could run much
faster than the old woman and the
old man, who could not run very
fast at all, and he soon left
them far behind.

On his way across a grassy field
he met a cow.
"Stop! Stop!" mooed the cow. "You
look good enough to eat to me."
The gingerbread man laughed. "I
have run away from a little old
man and a little old woman and
I will run away from you too,"
he said. And he did.

He ran through a
tiny gap in the
hedge, and though
the cow tried,
she could not
follow him.

As he ran through a farmyard he
was chased by a dog.
"Stop! Stop!" barked the dog.
"You look good enough to eat to
me."

The gingerbread man laughed. "I have run away from a little old man, a little old woman, and a cow, and I will run away from you too." And he did. He ran under the farmyard gate and when the dog tried to follow he got stuck.

In the leafy lane he met a horse.
"Stop! Stop!" neighed the horse.
"You look good enough to eat to me."
The gingerbread man laughed. "I have run away from a little old man, a little old woman, a cow and a dog, and I will run away from you too." And he did.

He dodged between
the horse's legs
to confuse him
and the horse did
not see which way
he went.

The gingerbread man was just
thinking how clever he was when
he met a fox. The fox looked
at the gingerbread man and
licked his lips hungrily, but
he said nothing.

The gingerbread man said, "You will never catch me. I have run away from a little old man, a little old woman, a dog and a cow and a horse, and I will run away from you too."

"There is no need to run away from ME," said the sly, old fox. "I do not want to catch you. Let us just walk along together."

And so they did.

Presently they came to a river.
"What shall I do?" asked the
gingerbread man. "I cannot swim."
"That's no problem," said the fox,
"I can. If you sit on my tail
I will take you across to the
other side."

And so the little gingerbread man did just that. When they reached the middle of the river, the fox said. "The water is getting deep. You had better move up onto my nose or you will get wet."

The gingerbread
man did not want
to get wet so he
walked along the
fox's back until
he came to his
nose.

"I can see where
we are going now,"
he laughed. "This
is fun."

But, as soon as they reached the far bank, the fox threw back his head, and as the gingerbread man fell, he caught him in his mouth and gobbled him up.

"One has to be clever to catch a gingerbread man," laughed the sly old fox.

All these appear in the pages of
the story. Can you find them?

little old man

little old woman

rocking chair

gingerbread man

cow

dog

horse

fox

Use the pictures to tell the story
in your own words, and then draw
your own pictures.

The Three Billy-Goats Gruff

It had been a long winter with
lots of snow. Food had been hard
to find and the Three Billy-goats
Gruff were very thin. But now the
snow had gone from the pasture
and the grass was looking fresh
and green.

"I shall go to the top pasture
today," said First Billy-goat Gruff,
who was also the smallest. "The
grass is always much greener and
sweeter up there."

"Take care the troll does not
catch you," said his brothers who
were playing at pushing with their
horns. "We will follow you later."

To get to the top pasture the three Billy-goats Gruff had to cross a stream. The water was deep and cold and the only way over it was by the humpy-backed bridge.

Underneath the bridge, in the dark and the damp, lived a bad-tempered troll. He had eyes as big as saucers and a nose as long and as sharp as a poker. Everyone was afraid of him, and there was nothing he liked better than eating goat for dinner.

The troll was splashing his feet
in the stream and trying to catch
a fish with his toes when he
heard, tip...tap...tip...tap...
above his head.

"Who is that walking over MY
bridge?" he shouted

"It is I," called First Billy-goat
Gruff, trembling like a leaf.
"Then I will have you for my
dinner," roared the troll.
"Please don't do that," pleaded
First Billy-goat Gruff. "I am
very small and thin. One mouthful
and I would be gone. My brother
is much fatter than I."

"Then I will wait, and have HIM for my dinner instead of you," said the troll. "Be on your way before I change my mind."

First Billy-goat Gruff did not need telling twice. He skipped off to the pasture as fast as his legs would take him.

The bad-tempered troll went back under the bridge and teased the toads while he waited for his dinner to come. Presently, he heard more footsteps tapping across the bridge ... tip ... tap ... tip ... tap "Who is that walking over MY bridge?" he shouted.

"It is I," called Second Billy-goat Gruff.

"Then I will have you for my dinner," roared the troll.

"Please don't do that," pleaded Second Billy-goat Gruff. "It has been a long hard winter. I am still very bony and thin. My brother will be coming this way soon, he is much fatter than I."

"Then I will wait and have HIM
for my dinner instead of you,"
said the troll. "Be on your way
before I change my mind."
Second Billy-goat Gruff did not
need to be told twice either,
and quickly joined First Billy-goat
Gruff in the top pasture.

The troll sat under the bridge in the damp and the dark and waited. He was getting very hungry and more and more bad-tempered. He tried to catch a fish but couldn't. And he couldn't tease the toads because they had hidden.

He waited and waited. He waited
a very long time, but at last,
he heard footsteps above his head.
Tip . . . tap . . . tip . . . tap . . . tip . . . tap
"Who is that walking over MY
bridge?" he shouted.

"It is I!" called Third Billy-goat
Gruff.

"Then I am coming to eat you!" roared the troll.
"Come and try!" shouted Third Billy-goat Gruff.

Out rushed the troll. What a surprise he had.

133

The Third Billy-goat Gruff was
also the largest Billy-goat Gruff.
He had long curly horns on his
head, and a beard hanging from
his chin. He was afraid of
no one.

He caught the troll with his
horns and tossed him up into the
air. Up...up...up went the troll.
And then, down...down...down
came the troll.

Third Billy-goat Gruff tossed him again. He tossed him so high he almost reached the moon.

Then while the troll was tumbling through the sky, Third Billy-goat Gruff went to the top pasture and joined his brothers.
The troll NEVER came back and from that day onwards it was quite safe to cross the humpy-backed bridge.

All these appear in the pages of
the story. Can you find them?

Second Billy-goat Gruff

First Billy-goat Gruff

troll

Third Billy-goat Gruff

moon

bridge

toad

stream

Use the pictures to tell the story
in your own words, and then draw
your own pictures.

Chicken Licken

Chicken Licken was playing in the
farmyard one day when an acorn
fell on his head.

"Ouch" was the first thing Chicken
Licken said. The second thing he
said was, "The sky is falling. I
must run and tell the King."

On the way across the farmyard,
he bumped into Henny Penny.
"Where are you going in such a
hurry?" asked Henny Penny as they
both picked themselves up.
"A piece of the sky has just
fallen on my head. I am going
to tell the King," said Chicken
Licken.

"I will go with you," said Henny Penny.

Cocky Locky was sitting on the
farmyard fence practising his crow.
"Where are you going in such a
hurry?" he asked in the middle
of a cock-a-doodle-do.
"We are going to tell the King
the sky is falling," said Chicken
Licken and Henny Penny, without
stopping.

"Then I will go
with you," said
Cocky Locky and
ran to catch up with them.

Ducky Lucky was swimming on the pond.

"Where is everyone going in such a hurry?" she asked.

"We are going to tell the King the sky is falling," said Chicken Licken, Henny Penny and Cocky Locky, without stopping.

"Wait for me!" said Ducky Lucky.
"I will go with you." She
swam to the edge of the pond
and waddled after them.

Drakey Lakey was looking at
himself in a puddle.
"Why is everyone in such a hurry?"
he asked, as they splashed through
the puddle one after the other.

"The sky is falling. We must tell
the King," said Chicken Licken,
Henny Penny, Cocky Locky and Ducky
Lucky, without stopping.

"That sounds serious," said Drakey
Lakey, "I will go with you."

Goosey Loosey was looking for worms
in the mud.
"Where is everyone going in such
a hurry?" he asked.
"The sky is falling. We are on
our way to tell the King," said
Chicken Licken, Henny Penny, Cocky
Locky, Ducky Lucky and Drakey
Lakey, without stopping.

"I will go with
you," said Goosey
Loosey, spreading
his great white
wings. "I can
look for worms
later."

Turkey Lurkey was
scratching about
in the barn.
"Where are you
all going in such
a hurry?" he asked.
"To tell the King
the sky is falling,"
said Chicken Licken, Henny Penny,
Cocky Locky, Ducky Lucky, Drakey
Lakey and Goosey Loosey, without
stopping.

"Then I will go with you," said
Turkey Lurkey. "I have always
wanted to see the King."

Chicken Licken, Henny Penny, Cocky Locky, Ducky Lucky, Drakey Lakey, Goosey Loosey and Turkey Lurkey were hurrying along the footpath through the wood when they met Foxy Loxy.

"Where are you all going in such
a hurry?" asked Foxy Loxy.
"To tell the King the sky is
falling," they said, without
stopping.
"Then follow me," said Foxy Loxy,
"I know a short cut to the King's
palace."

But Foxy Loxy did not lead Chicken Licken, Henny Penny, Cocky Locky, Ducky Lucky, Drakey Lakey, Goosey Loosey and Turkey Lurkey to the palace. He led them to his own den where his family were waiting for him to bring them dinner.

And that was the end of Chicken
Licken, Henny Penny, Cocky Locky,
Ducky Lucky, Drakey Lakey, Goosey
Loosey and Turkey Lurkey. They
never did get to the palace to
tell the King that a piece of
the sky had fallen on Chicken
Licken's head.

All these appear in the pages of
the story. Can you find them?

Chicken Licken

Henny Penny

Cocky Locky

Ducky Lucky

Goosey Loosey

Drakey Lakey

Turkey Lurkey

Foxy Loxy

Use the pictures to tell the story
in your own words, and then draw
your own pictures.

Foolish Jack

Foolish Jack always did as he was told whether it made sense or not. Sometimes he made some very foolish mistakes because what makes sense one day does not always make sense the next day.

One morning Jack's mother woke him
early, and said,
"There is very little food left in
the cupboard. You must find work
and bring home a wage or we will
starve."

Jack found work with a farmer. He fed the pigs, and the cows and the chickens.

At the end of the day the farmer gave him a penny. "Take that home to your mother," he said.

Jack had never had money of his own before. He did not know how to look after it. He tossed the penny into the air and caught it. He rolled it along a wall. And he lost it. He was rolling it along the road when it fell into a crack. He tried to get it out but the crack was deep and his fingers were short. He had to leave the penny where it was and go home without it.

"What wage did the farmer give you?"
asked his mother when he got home.

"A penny," said Jack proudly.

"Where is it?" asked his mother.

"In a crack in the road," said
Jack, and he told her what had
happened.

"You silly boy!" she said. "You
should have put it in your pocket.
It would have been safe there."

The next day Jack went to work at the dairy. He helped carry the heavy buckets of milk. The dairy-maid gave him a jug of milk as his wage.

Jack remembered what his mother had said about the penny and when it was time to go home he put the jug of milk in his pocket.

"Where are your wages?" asked his
mother as soon as he got home.
"In my pocket of course," said Jack.
His mother was very cross when she
saw the empty jug and the mess the
milk had made.
"You silly boy!" she said. "You
should have balanced the jug on your
head then the milk would not have
spilt."

Next day Jack helped the farmer's wife clean the farmhouse windows. She gave him a piece of cream cheese to take home.

"I will carry my wage properly this time," said Jack, and he balanced the cheese on his head.

He walked home
very slowly. He
did not want the
cheese to fall.
It had been a
very hot day and
the sun was still
shining. Presently
the cheese began
to melt. It ran
into Jack's hair
and down his face.
It made him very
sticky.

"I am home mother," he called when
he got to the door. "I did as
you told me. I put my wages on
my head."
"You silly boy!" said his mother as
she washed him clean. "You should
have wrapped the cheese in leaves
and carried it in your hands then
it would not have melted."
Jack did not say anything. He
could not. His mouth was full of
soap.

The next day Jack helped clean out
the stables. The stable-man gave
him one of the stable cats. When
it was time to go home Jack
wrapped the cat in leaves as though
it was a piece of cheese.

The cat did not
like being wrapped
in leaves. It
struggled and
scratched until it
was free.

"Come back!" shouted
Jack as the cat
ran away. But the
cat would not come
back. Jack could
not catch it
either and he had
to go home without
it.

"Where is the cat now?" asked Jack's mother, as she bathed and bandaged his scratches.

"At the top of a tree," said Jack.

"You silly boy!" said his mother. "You should have tied a piece of string round its neck and led it home then it would not have run away."

Jack remembered his mother's words of advice next day, when the butcher paid him with a joint of meat. He tied a string round that, and pulled that home behind him. It was stolen by a hungry dog when Jack was not looking.

Jack's mother looked at the empty string and sighed. Jack looked at the empty string and scratched his head.

"There was a joint of meat on the end of that string when I started for home," he said.

"You silly boy!" said his mother. "You should have carried it on your shoulder. It would have been safe there."

The next day Jack's wages was a goat.

"I know what I must do with you. I must carry you on my shoulder," said Jack. The goat was nearly as big as Jack and it was very heavy.

In the town where Jack lived there
was a girl who had never smiled.
Her rich father had promised a
reward to anyone who could make he
laugh. Lots of people had tried
but she did not laugh until the
day she saw Jack carrying the goat
home on his shoulder.

The sight of Jack wearing a goat round his neck like a scarf was enough to make anyone laugh. The little girl laughed until the tears rolled down her cheeks.

Jack received a fine reward and from that day onwards he and his mother always had enough to eat. Perhaps Jack was not as foolish as he seemed.

All these appear in the pages
of the story. Can you find them?

Jack

Mother

cheese

penny

washtub

cat

donkey

girl

Use the pictures to tell the story
in your own words, and then draw
your own pictures.

Little Red Hen

Little Red Hen lived with her three
friends in a house beside a muddy
pool. Little Red Hen was always
busy and it was she who kept the
house neat and tidy.

"Duck spends too much time swimming.
Pig spends too much time wallowing.
Cat spends too much time sleeping,"
she would cluck crossly as she
swept and dusted and cleaned.
"But I like swimming," said Duck.
"I would rather swim on the pond
than do anything else."

"And I like wallowing," said Pig.
"I would rather wallow in the mud
than do anything else."

"And I like sleeping," said Cat.
"I would rather sleep in the sun
than do anything else."

One day, when
Little Red Hen
was scratching
about in the
garden looking
for worms, she
found some grains
of wheat.
"Who will help
me plant these
grains of wheat?"
she called to
her three friends.

"Not I," quacked Duck. "I am going for a swim."

"Not I," grunted Pig. "I am going for a wallow."

"Not I," miaowed Cat. "I am too sleepy."

"Then I will plant them myself," said Little Red Hen.

And she did.

She planted the grains in a corner
of the garden. She watered them
and they began to grow. Each day
the shoots grew a little taller.
The sun shone on the growing wheat
and ripened it, and one day, it
was ready to cut.
"Who will help me cut the wheat?"
called Little Red Hen.

"Not I," quacked Duck. "I am going for a swim."

"Not I," grunted Pig. "I have found a new patch of mud."

"Not I," miaowed Cat. "I am looking for a place to sleep."

"Then I will cut it myself," said Little Red Hen. And she did. She sharpened the blade and cut the stems of wheat. When they were cut she gathered them together and made them into a large bundle with all the plump golden ears at one end. When she was finished she called her friends.

"Who will help me thresh the wheat?" she asked.

"Not I," quacked Duck, and dipped her head into the pond.

"Not I," grunted Pig, and rolled over in the mud.

"Not I," miaowed Cat, and curled up on top of the wall.

"Then I will thresh it myself,"
said Little Red Hen.
And she did.
It was very hard work. It made
her puff and it made her feel
tired. But at last all the grains
had fallen from the ears. She
gathered them up and put them into
a basket.
"Who will take the grains of wheat
to the mill to be ground?" she
called.

"Not I," quacked Duck.
"Not I," grunted Pig.
"Not I," miaowed Cat.
"Then I will take
them to the mill
myself," said
Little Red Hen.
And she did.
The mill stood on
top of a hill so
that the wind
could blow the
sails. It was a
long steep climb.
Little Red Hen was
very tired by the
time she got there.

The miller ground
the wheat into
flour for her and
poured it into a
strong linen bag.
Little Red Hen
put the linen bag
into the basket
and carried it
home.

The next morning, when Little Red
Hen, Duck, Pig and Cat, were having
breakfast, Little Red Hen said,
"Who will help me bake a loaf of
bread today?"
"Not I," quacked Duck, and waddled
outside quickly. "I want to swim
on the pond."

"Not I," grunted Pig, gulping his toast. "I want to wallow in the mud."

"Not I," miaowed Cat, with a lazy yawn. "I want to sleep in the sun."

"Then I will bake it myself," said Little Red Hen.

And she did.

She chopped some wood. She lit
the fire. She made the flour into
dough. She put the dough into a
tin. She put the tin into the
oven. And then she waited.
Soon a delicious smell wafted
through the kitchen.

When the bread was cooked Little
Red Hen took it from the oven and
put it on the windowsill to cool.
"Who will help me eat my loaf of
brown crusty bread?" she called.

"I will," quacked Duck.

"I will," grunted Pig.

"I will," miaowed Cat.

"You are all wrong," said Little Red Hen. "I found the grains of wheat. I planted them. I looked after the wheat. I watered it. I cut it. I threshed it. I carried it to the mill. I made it into bread. So I am going to eat it." And she did, EVERY crumb.

All these appear in the pages
of the story. Can you find them?

red hen

duck

cat

pig

wheat grain

mill

flour

bread

Use the pictures to tell the story in your own words, and then draw your own pictures.